THE
PRIVATE EYES CLUB
TREASURY
●●●●●●●●●●●●●●●●●●●●●●●●●●●
Three Great
Mysteries

written and illustrated by
Crosby Bonsall

BARNES
&NOBLE
B O O K S
N E W   Y O R K

Contents

The Case of the Hungry Stranger

The Case of the Cat's Meow

The Case of the Double Cross

HarperCollins®, ®, Harper Trophy®, and I Can Read Book®
are trademarks of HarperCollins Publishers Inc.

The Private Eyes Club Treasury
The Case of the Hungry Stranger
Copyright © 1963, 1992 by Crosby Bonsall
The Case of the Cat's Meow
Copyright © 1965 by Crosby Bonsall
The Case of the Double Cross
Copyright © 1980 by Crosby Bonsall

ISBN 07607-03698

An I Can Read Book®

THE CASE OF THE
Hungry Stranger

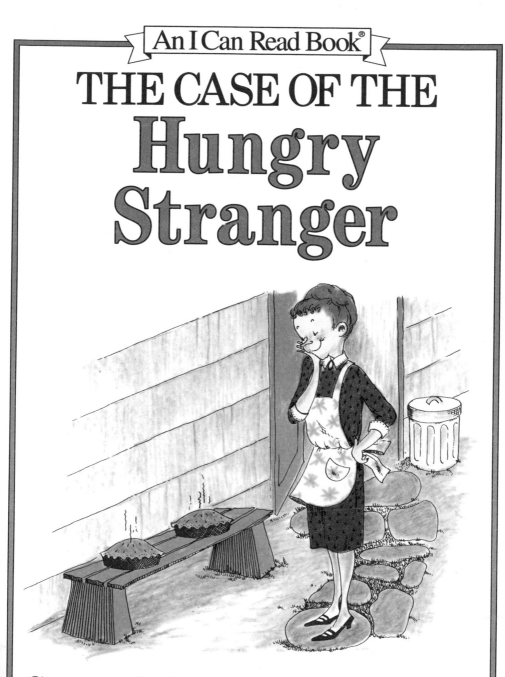

Story and pictures by Crosby Bonsall

HarperTrophy
A Division of HarperCollins*Publishers*

HarperCollins®, ▲®, and I Can Read Book®
are trademarks of HarperCollins Publishers Inc.

THE CASE OF THE HUNGRY STRANGER

Library of Congress Cataloging-in-Publication Data
Bonsall, Crosby Newell, date
     The case of the hungry stranger / story and pictures by Crosby
Bonsall. — Newly illustrated ed.
         p.   cm. — (An I can read book)
     Summary: Wizard and his friends are clueless when they are sent on
the trail of a blueberry pie thief, until Wizard hits on a plan that
is sure to nab the sweet-toothed pilferer.
     ISBN 0-06-444026-5 (pbk.)
     [1. Mystery and detective stories.]   I. Title.   II. Series.
PZ7.B64265Cas   1992b   91-14365
[E]—dc20   CIP
                                                              AC

New Harper Trophy edition, 1992.

They all sat

in the clubhouse.

Wizard and Tubby,

Skinny and Snitch.

6

Wizard was the leader.

Tubby was his pal.

Skinny was his pal.

Snitch was his little brother.

Wizard knew a lot,

so he was called Wizard.

Tubby ate a lot,

so he was called Tubby.

8

Skinny did not eat a lot,

so he was called Skinny.

Snitch was called Snitch

because he told on his brother.

Sometimes.

The clubhouse was under a tree,

by a brook,

near a fence,

in Wizard's backyard.

10

There was an old sign on the door.

It said: NO GIRLS

There was a new sign on the door.

It said: THE WIZARD

PRIVATE EYE

"What is a private eye?"

asked Snitch.

"I am a private eye," said Wizard.

"I find things."

"I lost a penny once," said Snitch.

Wizard said, "I don't find lost things.

I find things that have been taken.

If someone took your penny,

I would find out who took it

and get it back for you."

"Free?" asked Snitch.

"For a nickel," said Wizard.

"Let it stay lost," said Snitch.

"You have to be sharp

to be a private eye," Wizard said.

"You have to keep your eyes open."

He looked at Snitch.

"You have to keep your mouth closed."

14

Mrs. Meech, the lady next door,

ran across the yard.

"Which one of you ate

my blueberry pie?" she asked.

15

They all looked at Tubby.

Mrs. Meech said,

"I baked two pies.

I put them out to cool.

And someone ate one.

All that is left is an empty pie plate."

"I didn't eat it," said Wizard.

"I didn't eat it," said Tubby.

"I didn't eat it," said Skinny.

"I didn't eat it," said Snitch.

"Cross my heart."

Mrs. Meech said,

"I need a private eye."

"You came to the right place,"

said Wizard.

"We'll find out

who ate the pie."

"I am sure you will," said Mrs. Meech.

18

Wizard looked at the boys.

"We will start right here," he said.

"Tubby, where were you

before you came here?"

19

"I went to the store

for a loaf of bread for Mom,"

Tubby said.

"I got some cookies for me, too."

"Where were you, Skinny?"

asked Wizard.

"I was watching my little sister

while my mother hung up the clothes,"

Skinny said.

"Where were you, Snitch?"

asked Wizard.

21

Snitch looked funny.

"I was with you," he said.

Now Wizard looked funny.

"Where were YOU, Wizard?"

asked Tubby and Skinny.

"I'll tell," said Snitch.

"It's funny.

Mom was trying on her new hat."

"That's not so funny,"

said Tubby and Skinny.

23

"She was trying it on Wizard,"
cried Snitch.

"THAT'S FUNNY!"

cried Tubby and Skinny.

"Come on, men," Wizard said.

"We have to look

for fingerprints, and footprints,

and anything else that will help us."

They climbed the fence.

They walked across the grass.

They stopped at Mrs. Meech's
back door.

The pie plate was on a bench.

It was empty, all right.

"Here's a footprint," yelled Skinny.

"It looks new," Wizard said.

Then he looked at Skinny's feet.

"It's YOUR footprint," he yelled.

"You just made it!"

Tubby was looking at

the open cellar door.

"Maybe he went down here,"

he said.

"I'll go look."

The cellar was very dark.

It was damp and still.

Tubby fell over something.

It was soft. It moved.

It seemed to grab him.

"Help!" cried Tubby.

"I've got him!"

29

Mrs. Meech put on the light.

And there was Tubby

all tied up in the garden hose.

"You're a dope,"

said Wizard.

Outside, Wizard had a few things

to say to all of them.

"We are not getting very far

with this case," he said.

"Hey, here's a pie crumb," yelled Snitch.

"That means he went that way,"

cried Wizard.

"Let's go."

They followed the crumbs

across the grass,

up to the fence.

They saw the crumbs again

across the brook.

"Don't make a sound,"

said Wizard. "I think we've got him."

Tubby ate a cookie.

But he did not make a sound.

34

The trail led to the tree

and then to the door

of the clubhouse.

"S-sh," said Wizard,

"I'll open the door fast.

We'll catch him red-handed!"

There was no one there.

"Shucks, he got away,"

said Skinny.

"We almost had him," said Tubby.

He ate another cookie.

Some cookie crumbs fell

on the grass.

They all looked at the crumbs.

"Those were cookie crumbs

we followed," Wizard said.

"Tubby's old cookie crumbs,"

said Skinny.

"We must find out who did it,"
Wizard said.
"We can't be private eyes
if we don't find out
who ate the blueberry pie,"
said Skinny.

"Blueberry pie," said Wizard.

"Blueberry pie," said Wizard again.

"Hey, let me see your teeth."

"Why?" asked Tubby.

"Just let me see your teeth," said Wizard.

"And you can see mine."

"What do teeth

have to do with it?"

Skinny asked.

"I lost one," said Snitch.

"Does that count?"

"No," said Wizard.

"But if we had eaten

that blueberry pie,

our teeth would be blue!"

"And our teeth aren't blue,"

cried Tubby and Skinny.

"I think the one I lost was blue,"

said Snitch.

"Let's each go out alone,"
said Wizard, "and look for
someone with blue teeth."

42

They went up and down the block.

They went to each house.

They smiled and they smiled.

Snitch smiled at the mailman.

The mailman smiled back.

But his teeth were not blue.

43

Tubby smiled at

the ice-cream man.

The ice-cream man smiled back.

But his teeth were not blue.

And Tubby got an ice-cream cone.

Skinny smiled at

the paper boy.

The paper boy smiled back.

But his teeth were not blue.

45

Wizard smiled at

the policeman.

The policeman smiled back.

Of course his teeth were not blue!

Wizard and Tubby and Skinny

met back at the clubhouse.

"I didn't see one blue tooth,"

Skinny said.

"Where's Snitch?" asked Wizard.

No one knew.

"I told Mom I'd watch him,"

Wizard said.

"Let's go look for him."

But they didn't have to look.

Snitch came running

across the yard.

"Hurry," he said. "Hurry!

I have found the blue teeth!"

They all ran after Snitch.

They jumped across the brook.

They climbed the fence.

They ran across the grass.

Mrs. Meech was weeding.

She looked up and smiled.

Every one of her teeth was blue!

"Aw, Snitch," said Wizard.

"Her teeth are blue," said Snitch.

"They are indeed, Snitch,"

said Mrs. Meech.

"I had a dish of blueberries

for my lunch."

Back at the clubhouse

Wizard had a few things to say to Snitch.

"But you said to look for

blue teeth," Snitch said.

"Not Mrs. Meech's blue teeth,"

yelled Wizard.

Just then a dog ran

through a hole under the fence.

He jumped over the brook

and sat down beside them.

"Hey, he's been with us all day,"
Snitch said.

"He's a nice dog," said Skinny.

"Does he want a cookie?" asked Tubby.

54

The dog ran to Wizard.

He wagged his tail

and sat down.

Wizard smiled at the dog.

The dog smiled back at Wizard.

Then Wizard yelled.

Then they were all yelling.

The dog was barking.

He was jumping around.

And he was smiling.

56

The dog was smiling

a deep blue smile.

A blueberry pie smile.

"The case is closed," Wizard said.

"Here's our pie-eater.

Let's take him to Mrs. Meech."

58

The dog smiled his deep blue smile

at Mrs. Meech.

"You did a good job, boys,"

Mrs. Meech said.

"Now we're really private eyes,"

Wizard told her.

59

Someone cried, "Mop! Mop!"

A girl walked across the grass.

"There you are, Mop,"

she said to the dog.

"Where have you been all day?"

The dog just smiled.

But Wizard told her.

Tubby told her.

Skinny told her.

And Snitch told her.

He always told.

61

Mrs. Meech said,

"Would you like it? The blueberry pie

Mop didn't eat?"

Tubby was the first to say "Yes."

62

They took the pie

to the clubhouse.

Mop and the girl came, too.

The girl's name was Marigold.

She sat on the grass with them

and ate blueberry pie.

63

And they all smiled.

And each one of them smiled

a deep blue smile.

64

An I Can Read Book®

THE CASE OF THE
Cat's Meow

by Crosby Bonsall

HarperTrophy
A Division of HarperCollinsPublishers

HarperCollins®, 🏠®, and I Can Read Book®
are trademarks of HarperCollins Publishers Inc.

The Case of the Cat's Meow

Library of Congress Catalog Card Number: 65-11451
ISBN 0-06-444017-6 (pbk.)
First Harper Trophy edition, 1978.

for my mother EMN

for my sister MNP

and

for Midnight CAT

Snitch was yelling.

He was pulling a wagon

with a funny thing in it.

And he was yelling.

"Stop yelling,"

yelled his brother, Wizard.

"Stop yelling,"

yelled his friend Skinny.

"Stop yelling,"

yelled his friend Tubby.

8

Snitch stopped yelling.

It was very quiet.

The little noise in the wagon

sounded like a loud cry.

"MEOW!"

There, in an old bird cage,

sat Mildred.

Mildred was Snitch's cat.

"I'm keeping her safe," Snitch said.

"Somebody might steal her."

10

"Who wants old Mildred?" Tubby said.

"She's dumb."

"She's no fun," Skinny said.

"She makes too much noise,"
Wizard said.

"She's nice!" Snitch yelled.

"I love Mildred!"

"Nobody is going to steal Mildred,"

Wizard said. "We are private eyes.

We have our own clubhouse.

We have a sign on the door.

Nobody will steal anything.

Take my word for it."

"We can catch anybody now,"
Tubby said. "We have an alarm."

"What alarm?" Snitch asked.

"The alarm we just put in,"
Skinny said. "Step over this string."

13

"See," Wizard said, "if anybody comes sneaking around here, he will trip over this string. That will pull this pail of water down on his head. Then the string on the pail handle will ring this bell."

"And it will ring and ring and ring," Snitch cried. "And we will catch whoever wants to steal Mildred."

"Nobody wants to steal Mildred," Wizard said. "Take my word for it."

Snitch started to yell.

"Come on," said Wizard.

"It's almost time for supper."

"I knew it must be," Tubby said.

They stepped over the string.

Nobody wanted to set off the alarm.

16

When Snitch and Wizard got home,

Mildred ran up the back steps.

She ran in the little door

in the big door

that was her door.

"She's nice," Snitch said.

"I love Mildred."

But did Mildred love Snitch?

The next morning she didn't come

when Snitch called her.

He called and called and called.

18

Wizard looked out the window.

"Somebody stole Mildred,"

Snitch yelled.

"Nobody stole Mildred," Wizard said.

"Take my word for it."

But he came down in a hurry.

"I'll call Skinny and Tubby,"
Wizard said.

"They will help us find Mildred."

"Somebody stole her," Snitch said.

And he started to yell.

The boys looked for Mildred
all that day.

"Anybody seen a dumb cat?"
Tubby asked.

"Anybody seen a cat?"

Skinny asked.

"She doesn't do much."

"Anybody seen a noisy cat?"

Wizard asked.

23

"Have you seen my cat Mildred?"

Snitch asked.

"She's soft and she's nice.

And I love her."

But he did not find Mildred.

Nobody found Mildred.

Nobody had even seen Mildred.

Back at the clubhouse Wizard said,
"We are not very good private eyes
if we can't find Mildred."
"But how can we?" Skinny asked.
"Food!" Tubby said.
"Mildred has to eat."

25

"That's a good idea," said Wizard.

"Tonight we'll put food in the yard.

If Mildred is hungry, she'll come home."

"She likes liver," Snitch said,

"and strawberry jelly. Without seeds."

"*I* like strawberry jelly," Tubby said.

Each of the boys

brought some food.

27

Next day they had cats, all right.

They had cats in the tree,

cats on the roof.

They had cats on the grass

and one cat

sitting on a stone

in the middle of the brook.

But no Mildred.

"Our plan was no good," Wizard said.

"How do we get rid of these cats?"

"I know!" Skinny cried. "Dogs!

Dogs will chase the cats away."

"They will scare Mildred,"

Snitch said.

"Mildred isn't here," Wizard said.

Snitch started to yell again.

30

The boys brought every dog
they could find on the block.

31

They got rid of the cats, all right.

But now they had dogs.

They had dogs in the tree,

dogs on the roof.

They had dogs on the grass

and one dog

sitting on a stone

in the middle of the brook.

And it took the rest of the day

to take the dogs home.

After supper Wizard called a meeting.
"We have to keep our eyes open
day and night," he said.
"Let's ask if we can sleep
in the yard tonight."

They went to bed

even before their bedtime.

They liked being outdoors.

It was warm.

The sky was full of stars.

Soon each of them was sound asleep.

And that was when the alarm went off.

The bell rang and rang.

Wizard was up first.

And then Skinny.

Tubby got stuck in his sleeping bag.

So he took it with him.

Wizard turned on his flashlight.

39

There was Snitch.

"I heard someone stealing Mildred,"
he said.

"You can't steal a cat
who is not here!" Wizard yelled.

But they all went into the house
for the rest of the night.

Next day Snitch told them something.

"Last night I put food

in Mildred's dish.

And now it's gone!"

Wizard was mad

because he had not thought

of Mildred's dish.

But he had a plan.

That night he put Mildred's dish

on a cookie tin filled with flour.

"Whoever is eating the food

will have to walk over the flour."

"And the white feet will leave

a trail we can follow," Skinny cried.

Next morning the food was gone.

But there were clear white paw prints

going down the steps.

43

Then the paw prints stopped.

"Shucks," Tubby cried,

"the flour didn't last long enough."

And Snitch started to yell.

"What will we do now?" Skinny asked.

"Try again tonight," Wizard said.

"And we will lock Mildred's door."

"Why?" asked Tubby.

"That cat is so noisy," Wizard said,

"she will cry if she can't get in."

"And we'll hear her," Tubby said.

"And the case will be solved."

"Then we'll be private ears,"

Skinny said.

That night the boys met on the porch.

"Now let's keep our eyes open,"

Wizard said.

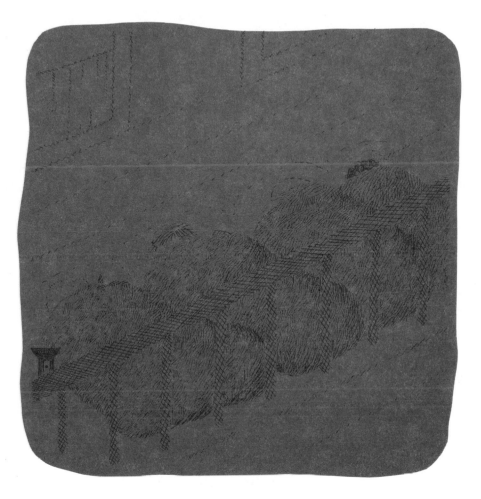

They went to bed early.

But the night was warm

and the sky was full of stars.

Soon they were sound asleep.

"What was that?" Tubby whispered.

"Just an old cat," Snitch said.

He started to go back to sleep.

49

"A CAT!" he shouted.

"It's Mildred! She is found!"

50

Wizard turned on his flashlight.

It was Mildred, all right.

But she was going away.

"Meow," she said as she left.

51

"Follow that cat," Wizard yelled.

Down the steps they ran,

over the grass, up to the clubhouse.

Mildred was one jump ahead of them.

One more jump took her
over the string.

The string that was part
of the alarm.

"Some alarm!" Wizard said.

"It sure doesn't catch cats!"

Each boy stepped over the string.

Mildred jumped into the basket

in the corner.

"Where's Mildred?" cried Snitch.

"I brought her supper."

"The case is solved," said Wizard.

"I told you nobody stole her."

Snitch ran over to the basket.

He started to yell again.

"MILDRED HAS KITTENS!"

"Oh, boy, I want one," Tubby cried.

"Me too," said Skinny.

"Don't forget me," Wizard said.

But Snitch had his arms
around the basket.

"Tubby said Mildred was dumb,"
Snitch said.

"Skinny said she was no fun.

Wizard said she made too much noise."

Well, they *had* said all those things.

Right then they changed their minds.

Mildred was nice. They loved her.

60

And so they waited for the kittens

to grow old enough

to leave their mother.

When they were old enough

Snitch gave a kitten

to each private eye.

"This is one case

I'm glad we solved," Skinny said.

"It's lucky," said Tubby,

"we're such good private eyes.

The alarm didn't help us."

"Snitch was the only one

we ever caught with it," Wizard said.

"Mildred will take care of us now,"

Snitch said.

"No, *my* cat will," said Tubby.

"No, *my* cat will," said Skinny.

"No, *my* cat will," said Wizard.

"You can take my word for it."

And Snitch was yelling again.

The Case of the
DOUBLE
CROSS

An I Can Read Book®

The Case of the
DOUBLE
CROSS

written and illustrated by
Crosby Bonsall

HarperTrophy
A Division of HarperCollins*Publishers*

HarperCollins®, 💾®, and I Can Read Book®
are trademarks of HarperCollins Publishers Inc.

The Case of the Double Cross
Copyright © 1980 by Crosby Bonsall
 For information address
HarperCollins Children's Books, a division of
HarperCollins Publishers, 10 East 53rd Street,
New York, NY 10022.

Library of Congress Cataloging-in-Publication Data
Bonsall, Crosby Newell.
    The case of the double cross.
    (An I can read book)
    Summary: Marigold concocts a mystery that
finally gets her and her friends into the
boys' private eye club.
    [1. Mystery and detective stories.
2. Clubs—Fiction.   3. Ciphers—Fiction]   I. Title.
PZ7.B64265Card   1980   [E]   80-7768
ISBN 0-06-020602-0
ISBN 0-06-020603-9 (lib. bdg.)
ISBN 0-06-444029-X (pbk.)

First Harper Trophy edition, 1982.

"Mean, mean, full of beans,

hope you get a hole in your jeans!"

"Mean, mean, full of beans,

hope you get a hole in your jeans!"

8

"It's old Marigold,"

Snitch told his brother Wizard

and their friends Skinny and Tubby.

9

The boys were private eyes.

They had their own clubhouse.

The sign on the door said:

NO GIRLS.

Wizard, the chief private eye,

put it up a long time ago.

10

Marigold and Gussie and Rosie

hated that sign.

Each day Marigold shouted,

"Mean, mean, full of beans,

hope you get a hole in your jeans!"

Each night she dreamed of ways

to join the club.

11

Marigold dreamed

she had a horse.

She let

the boys

ride it.

They begged her

to join their club.

Marigold dreamed

she saved the boys

from a terrible flood.

They begged her to join their club.

15

Marigold dreamed

she ran an ice-cream stand.

Marigold gave the boys

all the ice cream they could eat.

They begged her to join their club.

17

But THEY DIDN'T!

Marigold called Rosie and Gussie.

"I have a plan,"

she told them.

Next morning, a funny little man
with a long, long beard
handed Snitch a letter.

"For you and Wizard,

and Skinny and Tubby,"

mumbled the funny little man.

And he ran away.

"I can't read it," Wizard shouted.

"It's in code," Skinny said.

"Who gave it to you?" asked Tubby.

"A funny little man

with a long, long beard," Snitch said.

"We have to find him!" Wizard said.

"Let's go, men."

21

They looked everywhere.

But they did not find

the funny little man.

"Fine private eyes we are,"

Wizard groaned.

"Hey, there he is!" Snitch cried.

"Follow him!" Wizard shouted.

The funny little man

with the long, long beard

ran fast.

The boys ran after him.

Wizard passed him.

Snitch bumped into him.

26

Tubby almost grabbed him.

Skinny tripped over him.

"He ran away from me," Snitch wailed.

"We have to catch him," Skinny said,

"and make him tell us the code."

28

"Mean, mean, full of beans,

hope you get a hole in your jeans!"

"Marigold can help us catch him,"

Snitch told his brother.

Wizard scowled. "Get lost!

What do girls know?"

29

"What are you doing?" Marigold asked.

"Get lost," Wizard snapped.

"If I get lost, you'll be sorry,"

Marigold warned him.

"You heard me," Wizard growled.

"Here's the case,"

Wizard told the private eyes.

"We have a funny little man.

We have a letter in code.

We can't break the code.

We can't even find the man!"

31

"And there are four of us,

and only one of him." Tubby sighed.

"But he knows us," Snitch said.

"He gave the letter to me

and he knew our names."

"He's out to get us," Tubby cried.

Wizard scowled.

"We're looking for HIM," he shouted.

Snitch remembered something.

"But he found ME!"

"That's right," Wizard cried,

"we will let him find US.

We will set a trap!"

Snitch stood by the tree

where the funny little man

had given him the letter.

Tubby and Skinny and Wizard

hid behind the tree and waited.

At last they heard footsteps.

It was the funny little man.

The boys grabbed him.

"Yeow!"

yelled the funny little man.

"Get off my thumb!"

yelled the funny little man.

"HELP! HELP! HELP!"

Suddenly, two more
funny little men
came running.

Wizard chased a funny little man

who chased Tubby

who chased a funny little man

who chased Snitch

who chased a funny little man

who chased Wizard.

"One of those men is my sister,"

Skinny shouted,

"and the girls double-crossed us."

40

"It was a trick," Wizard groaned.

"And we fell for it," Tubby moaned.

"It was our TRAP," Marigold snapped.

"And you fell INTO it," Gussie yelled.

41

"You said ONE funny little man!"

Wizard glared at Snitch.

"I only counted one,"

Snitch whined.

"Don't yell at him,"

Marigold told Wizard.

"You can't even break the code.

BUT WE CAN!"

"Yikes," Wizard yelled,

"I forgot about the code!"

"Marigold said we'd be sorry,"

Tubby reminded him.

"Marigold said we were

full of beans," Tubby told them.

"They know the code." Skinny sighed.

"Yup," Wizard said.

"If we let them join our club,

they will tell us the code.

We will *have* to let them

join our club."

"We will let you join our club."

Wizard smiled.

"Let us WHAT?" Marigold demanded.

"Join our club," Tubby said.

"Your WHAT?" Gussie shouted.

"CLUB," Snitch screamed.

"Wait," Skinny yelled,

"I have broken the code!

I can read the letter!"

Dear Wizard, Snitch,
Tubby and Skinny
If you can read this
you are smarter
than we think you are.
IF YOU CAN'T
you need us
in your club.
Marigold
Gussie and
ROSie

Skinny held the side of the paper

with the writing toward the light.

Now he was looking at

the other side of the paper.

"It's written backward," he said,

and he read it out loud.

48

"Hold everything," Wizard shouted,
"we know the code,
so we don't need you!"

"Need us where?" Marigold asked.

"In our club," Wizard told her.

"We don't want to join
your dumb old club," Marigold said.

"You don't want to WHAT?"

Wizard shouted.

"Join your dumb old club,"

Gussie called out.

"Our WHAT?" Tubby demanded.

"Dumb old club," Rosie yelled.

"You stepped on my thumb,"

Rosie said.

"You're dumb," Gussie said.

"Anyway,

we are starting our own club,"

Marigold said.

"A club of their own!"

Wizard groaned.

"With their tricks,

and their traps," Tubby said.

"And their code," Skinny said.

"And their beards!" Snitch added.

"We *are* full of beans," Tubby said.

"Okay, okay!"

Wizard gave up.

"We will give them

another chance."

54

"You don't need your own club,"

Skinny said. "Join ours."

"NO!"

"You could use our clubhouse,"

Snitch told Marigold.

"NO!"

"I will share my cookies," Tubby said.

"NO!"

Wizard didn't say a word.

Wizard listened.

Then Wizard yelled,

"Okay! Okay!

We will take down the sign

that says NO GIRLS."

"Now you're talking," Marigold said.

"What shall we call our club?"

she asked.

"What's the matter with

Wizard, Private Eye?"

asked Wizard.

"Plenty," Marigold snapped.

"Wizard and Company?"

"Try again, Wizard,"
Marigold told him.

"How about Wizard and Girls?"
Snitch cried.

"I know," Skinny said. "Let's put
Wizard and Marigold together
and call ourselves The Wizmars."

61

"Now THAT'S fair," Marigold agreed.

"Shake," said Wizard.

And they did.

The Beginning